The Time Detectives

Terry Deary trained as an actor before turning to writing full time. He has many successful fiction and non-fiction children's books to his name, and is rarely out of the bestseller charts.

Other titles in the series:

The Witch of Nightmare Avenue
The Pirates of the Dark Park
The Princes of Terror Tower

The Time Detectives

Book 4

King Arthur's Bones

TERRY DEARY

Illustrated by Martin Remphry

ff

faber and faber

To Monica Murfin, librarian – but not like the one
in this book!

First published in 2000
by Faber and Faber Limited
3 Queen Square London WCIN 3AU

Origination: Miles Kelly Publishing
Printed in Italy

A CIP record for this book
is available from the British Library

ISBN 0-571-20122-9

iv

Contents

Chapter 1
King Arthur's Duckpool drama   1

Chapter 2
The king who had a kip   11

Chapter 3
A tartan terror in jam-jar glasses   21

Chapter 4
Ruling Romans and battered Brits   30

Chapter 5
A Bede and a border   38

Chapter 6
Nennius the ninny and other meddling monks   47

Chapter 7
Burials and bones   54

Chapter 8
Bombs and bagpipes   59

Chapter 9
The last great battle of Arthur's heirs   67

Chapter 10
Arthur's marvellous medal   78

Time trail   83

The Time Detectives
All about us

These are the files of the toughest team ever to tackle time-crime. We solve mysteries of the past, at last – and fast.

We are the Time Detectives.

My name is Bucket.

Katie Bucket. Commander of the Time Detectives.

And here is my squad. I wrote the secret files myself so you know they're true. Trust me...

#1

Number: TD 001

Name:

Katie Bucket

Appearance:

Gorgeous, beautiful and smart.
The slightly scruffy clothes and messy
hair are just a disguise to fool the
enemy.

Report:

Katie Bucket is the boss,
Grown-ups always make her cross.
She's the Time Detectives' leader.
Cos she's brainy they all need her!

Special skills:

Cunning, brave, quick-thinking. Really
I'm too modest to tell you just how
great I am.

Hobbies:

Playing football, wrestling snakes,
making trouble. (It's a full-time hobby
just being so popular!)

Favourite victim:

Miss Toon our teacher.

Catch-phrase:

"Trust me, I know what I'm doing."

Number: TD 002

Name:

Pete Plank

Appearance:

Like a brick wall only uglier. Big. Grown out of his clothes.

Report:

Big Pete Plank he is so strong,
Like the mighty ape, King Kong.
Went out one day in the rain,
Shame it washed away his brain.

Special skills:

Opening tin cans with his teeth and doors with his head. His face keeps vampire bats (and nosy kids) away.

Hobbies:

Eating, sleeping, eating. Favourite food: a pork-burger. (That's a pig in a bun, you understand.)

Catch-phrase:

"Uhh?"

Number: TD 003

Name:

Gary Grint

Appearance:

A weed with spectacles. Carries more gadgets in his anorak than a moon rocket.

Report:

Gary Grint, computer whiz,
Internetting is his biz.
Knows so much he's awful boring,
Talks till everyone is snoring.

Special skills:

Electronic gadgets, cracking codes, squeezing through small spaces – like letter-boxes.

Hobbies:

Train-spotting, chess, playing the violin (favourite tune: "The dying cat").

Catch-phrase:

"I'll bet you didn't know this!"

Number: TD 004

Name:

Mabel Tweed

Appearance:

So squeaky clean you could eat your dinner off her shining shoes. She's all posh frocks and white socks.

Report:

Mabel Tweed is so good,
So polite and sweet as pud.
Does her homework neat and quick,
Teacher's pet. She makes me sick!

Special skills:

Creeping, grovelling and being smarmy. I only let the lucky kid join TDs cos her dad's a millionaire.

Hobbies:

Tidying her room, polishing her bike, running errands for adults. Favourite place: at Miss Toon's feet.

Catch-phrase:

"Do excuse me."

Chapter 1
King Arthur's Duckpool drama

You may remember the headlines last Easter...

The Duckpool Daily News
Easter Monday Special Edition 55p

Local heroine saves the nation

Today this country honours a young heroine from here in Duckpool – the gallant girl who single-handedly performed the greatest act of courage since the Second World War.

KING ARTHUR MEDAL

But you want the truth behind the story. I'm one of the few who knows the whole truth. If you read this adventure in an Enid Blyton book you wouldn't believe it. But this is me, Katie Bucket, leader of the Time Detectives telling you this. Trust me. It all happened this way...

It all started with the school play. It was meant to be a bit of fun before the Easter holiday. Little did we know that we would end up in an ancient mystery, saving Britain from a deadly enemy and getting a medal for a Duckpool Time Detective.

"This term we'll do the story of King Arthur and the Knights of the Round Table," Miss Toon our teacher told us.

"Do excuse me, Miss," Mabel Tweed, the millionaire mayor of Duckpool's daughter asked. "But are there any good parts for girls?" She shook her golden ringlets and brushed a speck of dust off her frilled white dress.

"Some of the best parts in the play are for girls," our teacher told her.

"Yeah! You can be Arthur's horse, Mabel!" I told her with a smile.

Her mouth went as tight as a rat-trap and she glared at me. Her little white fists were clenched and she was making a growling noise in her throat.

"You'd be perfect as Morgan le Fey, Mabel," Miss Toon said quickly.

"She was the wicked witch wasn't she?" Gary Grint put in. Gary knows more old stories than my granny... and she was there when they happened!

Mabel's mouth opened as if she was about to object but Miss Toon explained, "She was the extremely beautiful... sorceress."

Mabel looked pleased. Pete Plank had to spoil it by asking, "If Mabel's the saucer then who's going to be the cup?" Pete is the nicest, kindest, most helpful boy in our class. He is also the tallest. Sadly he is not the brightest.

Mabel snapped at him, "Sorceress, you foolish boy with the brain of a bird."

Miss Toon stopped any arguments by taking us into the school hall to do some drama work. We tried acting out different parts of the old story and decided who would play what part.

I got the job of being King Arthur's boring wife, Guinevere. Gary was the brave, battling, brainless Lancelot. We were all surprised that Miss Toon chose Gary to be Lancelot. Gary is such a weed he makes a dandelion look like King Kong.

"Arthur was a giant of a man," Miss Toon explained. "So I think Pete Plank would be best for that part," she said.

"Uhh?" he exclaimed... he was pleased, surprised and confused.

Miserable Mabel just had to say, "Do excuse me, Miss Toon, but Plank can't even read!"

The teacher said quietly, "I will put his words on a tape and he can learn them. He may be a weak reader but he isn't stupid. Remember that will you please, Mabel?"

I felt like cheering her. And I've never cheered a teacher in my life!

Every evening after school we worked on that play. One of the best writers in the class turned it into a script. When we weren't practising on the stage then we were painting the scenery with Mr 'Potty' Potterton the headmaster or making costumes and swords with Miss Toon.

In the week before Easter we had sold every seat in the school hall. We weren't nervous, we were terrified! We were quite sure it was going to be the biggest disaster Duckpool had seen since Mr Potterton took us to the swimming pool in the park, dived in and lost his trunks.

But you don't want to hear about our play, do you? You want to see it, so here it is...

Scene 1
The Sword in the Stone

Narrator: Long ago, in the mists of time, there was a king of England called Uther Pendragon. King Uther had a son called Arthur. Merlin the Magician took Arthur away to protect him from Uther's enemies. Then Uther died. Merlin called all the great lords together.

Merlin: Uther is dead! We are all Uther-less!

Sir Kay: You've always been useless, Merlin!

Merlin: I have here a test. The next king is the person who pulls this sword from this stone!

Sir Kay: Easy-peasy! (But, when he tries...) Impossible! The sword is stuck fast. Have you glued it in with your chewing gum, Merlin?

Merlin: It is magic. Now let's get off to the tournament. Knights will do battle to entertain the ladies.

Narrator: Sir Kay had a young squire. Unknown to him the young squire was Arthur, secret son of the dead King Uther. As they made their way to the tournament Sir Kay suddenly realised something.

Sir Kay: Ah! Blow me. I've forgot me sword! Can't fight without a sword, Arthur.

Arthur: Well, you could... but you'd be chopped to pieces.

Sir Kay: Pop back to our castle and fetch me sword, young Arthur, there's a good lad.

Arthur: Okay, Sir Kay.

Narrator: But when Arthur got back to the castle he found it was locked.

Arthur: And everyone's gone off to the tournament! What will I do?

Narrator: He walked back and took a short cut through the churchyard. That's when he saw the magical sword in the stone.

And that was the first scene ended. It was a bit boring for me because I wasn't in it yet. I stood at the side of the stage and peered through a hole in the curtain.

The parents were grinning like hyenas in the zoo even though the star of the show had hardly even appeared yet. I guess they were skiving off work that afternoon and that's what made them so happy.

The lights glinted on the golden chain of Mayor Walter Tweed, Mabel's dad. Of course he had to be in the front row.

I looked over their heads to the back of the hall. It was dark there but I could just make out a figure. A figure so odd and shocking that I thought my heart had stopped beating. I clutched at my chest, and couldn't find my heart anywhere! I was sure I was dying.

I gave a gasping sort of croak and I knew dead people didn't do that so I was still alive. I rubbed my eyes and looked at the figure again. In the half-light I saw a dark shape. And, in its hand, there was a lance!

I was sure then that I was looking at one of King Arthur's knights... returned from the grave to haunt us!

Chapter 2
The king who had a kip

I pulled Pete Plank towards me and jabbed a finger at the hole in the curtain. "Look at that, Pete!"

"Uhh? It's a hole, Katie!" he said.

"I mean, look through the hole. Look at that figure at the back of the hall. It's a dark knight!" I hissed.

"Uhh? All nights are dark, Katie. Even I know that. If the nights weren't so dark they'd be days!" he explained.

Only his cardboard armour stopped me poking my wooden sword through his ear-hole to see if there was anything inside his skull. "Look at him, Pete. Just tell me what you see!"

He took his wooden sword, jabbed it at the hole till there was a good wide split and squinted through. "Uhh?" he grunted.

"Well? What can you see?" I asked.

"A big woman in a kilt with a window pole in her hand," he said.

"Eh?" I pulled him aside and looked again. Now that Pete had said that, I could see what he meant. It was just a woman holding the pole our caretaker uses to wind the top windows open. "It was an easy mistake to make," I said to Pete.

"A very easy mistake to make," Pete agreed.

"So don't make that mistake again," I warned him and walked off to check my make-up in the dressing-room. There was a list of the scenes on the wall so we knew where we were up to in the story. It was the part I thought was a little gruesome, violent and cruel. My favourite bit, in fact...

SCENE 2

Characters on stage:
Arthur, Merlin, Lady of the Lake, Knights.

Story: King Arthur walks by a lake and tells Merlin he has no sword.

Merlin points to the lake where a lady's hand is holding a sword out of the water. Arthur takes the sword. The lady says she will take her reward later.

Merlin tells Arthur that he will be killed by a person born on the first day of May. So Arthur sends for all the children born on that day; he loads them all onto a boat and sends it off to sea. The ship sinks but a knight's son, Mordred, survives.

The knights are upset at losing their children but blame Merlin rather than Arthur.

Then the scene ended with the knights' song that I could hear in the dressing-room...

At last it was time for the star of the show to appear. I put on my pointy hat – Miss Toon said it's called a 'wimple' – and waited for the curtains to open on my scene.

"Now Arthur's knights told the king that he should take a wife," Miss Toon went on with the story from the script...

Scene 3
The Round Table

Narrator: Arthur was quite keen on the
idea of getting married.

Arthur: Actually, lads, I quite like the
gorgeous Guinevere, daughter of King
Leodegrance! He has my Dad's old
Round Table.

Merlin: I have to warn you Arthur, I can
see into the future. If you marry her,
son, then she will run off with your
friend Sir Lancelot.

Arthur: Merlin, you are talking a load of
magical mouthwash. Go get me the
Guinevere girl!

Narrator: So Merlin went to the court of
King Leodegrance.

Merlin: Your Majesty, King Arthur
fancies your daughter. How about it?

King: Great idea. You'd like that,
wouldn't you pet?

Guinevere: I don't know, Dad. I've never
met the feller.

King: He's a lovely lad. Pulls swords
from stones and from lakes in his
spare time.

Then came my favourite part. The part where I met Arthur and he told me how beautiful I was.

I'm sure you'd like to read that bit, wouldn't you? Well, you're going to whether you like it or not because it's very important to remember.

Now, in case you hadn't guessed it... I wrote this wonderful script. It's a pity Pete had to be so spiteful about my beauty. He was jealous, of course.

We carried on with this brilliant play and the audience loved it. In scene four it was Mabel's turn to come back as the evil Morgan le Fey.

She steals Arthur's sword, Excalibur, and casts a spell on a knight to kill the king. (Larry Oliver played the part of the killer-knight and was a star except he took a long time to die. He rolled around on the stage for five minutes gasping and gurgling till he rolled close to the edge. I grabbed his arm and dragged him off.)

In the last scene Gary (as Lancelot) tries to run away with me. Pete (as Arthur) tries to have me burned at the stake. Mordred the traitor goes to war and poor Arthur is badly wounded. He ordered that his mighty sword should be thrown into the lake. (The lake was a blue sheet on the stage with Gloria Green lying underneath it! Her hand reaches through a hole in the sheet and takes it. Clever, eh?)

Then Arthur made his final speech. Pete was so good Mayor Tweed was almost in tears – just as well gold neck chains don't rust!

I do not die, my dearest friends,
I simply go to sleep.
So say farewell, and smile and laugh,
I hate to see you weep.

Some future day you British folk
Will face a fearsome foe.
Then I'll awake, I will return,
But for now I have to go!

The play ended and the audience cheered and roared and clapped. I think most of the cheers were for the writer, of course.

We lined up on the stage to take our bow. I looked over the audience towards the back of the hall to get a better look at the woman with the window pole.

And there she was... gone!

Chapter 3

A tartan terror in jam-jar glasses

The curtain finally fell after the show. The mayor, Walter Tweed, rose to his feet and made a speech. He said how brilliant his daughter Mabel had been as the evil Morgan. He even joked that Mabel was just as evil at home! The audience laughed till they were sick and his speech went on nearly as long as my play.

We tidied the stage and folded our clothes and finally got back to the classroom just before home time.

"I hope you all enjoy your Easter holiday," Miss Toon said. "I am sure you will miss school terribly," she smiled. There was a great groan from the class.

"And I will miss you just as much," she added.

Teachers lie too.

Miss Toon's classroom has a door with glass squares in the top half. But the glass is wibbly so you can only see shapes and colours of people passing by. Just at that moment I saw the shape of a knight with a lance.

"Miss Toon!" I hissed. "There's a strange woman following us! She was watching the play from the back of the hall and now she's outside the door! Call the police!"

Our teacher didn't look the least bit worried. In fact she looked as if it were all a joke. She walked to the door and opened it. The figure stood there.

"Come in, Miss Monument, and meet the actors," Miss Toon said.

The strange woman's colourless hair was cut in a fringe and her eyes peered through glasses like jam-jar bottoms.

She looked as pleased to see us as a rat is pleased to see a cat. She pulled a mud-brown cardigan around her wide chest.

The only colours I could see were in her tartan skirt. When she spoke she showed teeth like tombstones, large and grey. "I was interested in your play because I am desperate to find out about Arthur. The real Arthur." She spoke with a curious accent that I couldn't quite place.

"Miss Monument works in Duckpool Central Library," Miss Toon explained. "She found all the books that you used to write the play, Katie," she added.

I tried to smile at the fearsome woman but her tombstone teeth were bared as if she wanted to eat me.

"The play was a clever piece of nonsense, of course," the librarian said. "The Sword in the Stone, the Lady of the Lake and the knights in shining armour are all just old tales made up by poets. No, I am interested in finding the real King Arthur. But most of all I am keen to find out where he is sleeping now."

23

"So you can wake him? Is Britain in danger?" I asked.

But before I could answer the door opened and a little, dribbling infant child toddled in. "Pleathe, Mith, Mithter Potterton thent thith methage!" she said and put a message in Miss Toon's hand.

The teacher frowned. A sheet of paper was wrapped around a cassette tape. "It seems there's an urgent message. Mr Potterton wants us all to hear it before we go home. It's a recording from the local radio news about something that happened while we were performing the play. Something important..."

She took the tape and slipped it into a cassette player. We crowded round...

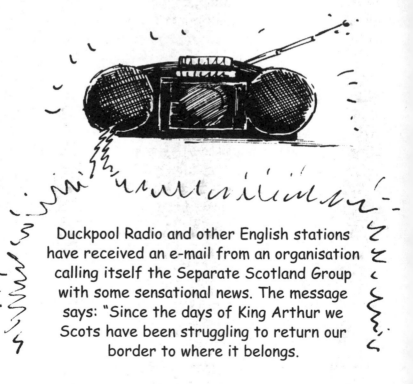

Duckpool Radio and other English stations have received an e-mail from an organisation calling itself the Separate Scotland Group with some sensational news. The message says: "Since the days of King Arthur we Scots have been struggling to return our border to where it belongs.

The true border is along the line of
Hadrian's Wall. Fifteen hundred years ago
we were driven back by your Arthur. Now
we are back. This time we will separate
Scotland and England for good. Do you
South Britons want to know what we mean?
You'll have to wait and see! But be warned.
Nothing and no-one will be able to stop
our mighty army!
Signed, Hamish McNasty."

The Prime Minister said today that he is
not taking the Separate Scotland Group
very seriously. He said, "If they try to
attack then we'll just have to wake old King
Arthur up to defend us again! Ho! Ho! Ho!"

The Prime Minister has refused to call in
the British army, saying there is no sign of
any invasion from north of the border. "And
anyway," he added, "the Scots are lovely
friendly people who wouldn't say boo to
a bagpipe!"

Many people are taking the threat more
seriously. Duckpool Town Council has
advised parents to keep children at home
and lock their doors until this threat is
lifted. Children still at school should leave
now... right now... and go home!

There was great bustle in the classroom as our classmates snatched up bags and books and raced for the door. Miss Toon tried to control them but it was a bit like a sandcastle trying to stop a watery wave. They flowed round her and out.

I was proud to see my Time Detectives stood firm.

"I am King Arthur!" Pete Plank said suddenly. "I have to awake and fight this fearsome foe!"

I shook him. "No. You are Pete Plank playing a part! You are also a Time Detective! If we're going to save Britain we need to find Arthur's resting-place!"

"I'll bet you didn't know this," Gary cut in. "But King Arthur is just a fairy tale, Katie. We can't waste time looking for a king who never was!"

"He's not a fairy tale!" Miss Monument said and her voice was a growl. "He's a legend."

"What's the difference?" Gary asked.

"Well, a legend is based on a true story," she explained.

"And there really was a King Arthur?" I asked.

26

"It seems some historians think there was a king called Arthur. I found this out when I collected the books for your play. I'm close to an answer. Did Arthur live? And, if so, where is he buried and is he just sleeping?"

"A case for the Time Detectives, my good woman," Mabel said.

"That's what I thought," Miss Monument nodded.

"Can we see what you've got in the library?" I asked her.

She frowned. "Of course. I need someone to look at it and bring fresh minds to crack the case. But there's not much time to lose. If the Scots are attacking we need to find Arthur and kill him as soon as we can."

"Kill him!" I exclaimed.

She turned her eyes on me and her smile froze. "Did I say 'kill' him? I meant 'wake' him. Silly me! If you can use your Time Detective skills to find him you will be doing my people a great service!"

"Let's start now," Mabel Tweed cut in, trying to take over as usual. "We can go to Duckpool Central Library tomorrow."

"It's closed on a Good Friday, Miss Smarty-knickers," I told her.

She tilted her little button nose in the air. "Do excuse me, you rather tatty-haired girl, but Daddy's the mayor and his council run the library. He'll have it opened specially for me," she said.

And that's how we found ourselves at the side door of the library that evening.

Gary had a school satchel with him. "She's right," he said. "I spent most of last night on the internet and I've a mass of research on the true story of Arthur."

"And where he's buried?" I asked.

"And where he's supposed to have been buried," Gary said. "But it's not all good news."

"Excuse me, round-faced little boy, but what's not good news?" Mabel Tweed asked. Her car had rolled up so quietly we hadn't heard her arrive.

"I'll tell you all inside," Gary said, "when we're all together."

Only Pete was late. Then with a roar of an engine and a puff of burning rubber a rider appeared. He was dressed in a shining black leather suit and a black helmet.

The rider tore off the helmet and grinned at us. "Pete!" I cried. "You're too young to ride a motorbike! The police would lock you up if they saw you."

He shrugged. "They can't see who's riding when I have this helmet on. I was helping Dad in his garage and I was going to be late. I had to bring it. I'm King Arthur and this is my horse."

"I'm Morgan le Fey," Mabel said sourly, "And I always travel in a Rolls Royce!"

The gleaming black bike was beautiful. It shone in the spring evening sunshine. Now that Pete was here we rang the bell at the side door and Miss Monument opened it. She was wearing her Duckpool Library badge... it read:

The inside of the library store room was dull and dusty. Dust even seemed to be gathering on Miss Monument's top lip. Either that or she was growing a moustache.

She turned her back and led the way into the gloom. Then she stopped and fixed me with those watery magnified eyes. "I'm desperate to find if there really is a sleeping Arthur," she said. "Desperate, I tell you! Desperate!"

It was going to be a fun afternoon.

Chapter 4
Ruling Romans and battered Brits

Mildred Monument's room was stuffed so full of books, newspapers and cardboard boxes, there was hardly room for the four Time Detectives and Miss Monument to turn around, let alone sit down. We crowded round a small table, lit by a weak light bulb while the ghosts of all the dead authors seemed to be watching us from the dark corners of the room.

The librarian uncovered a computer in the corner of the room, tapped in a few words and printed out a list of the books on King Arthur. "I'll be about ten minutes. Don't touch anything while I'm out!"

Whenever someone says that, I simply have to touch something, don't you? I picked up a newspaper from the table. I thought at first it was older than my grandad. The headline was so shocking...

The Duckpool Daily News

26th March   55p

BRITAIN AT WAR!

Duckpool Daily News today received a horrifying fax from the Separate Scotland Group. This secret organisation demanded that Scotland should be separated from England along the line of old Hadrian's Wall. But now the group's leader is furious that the British Prime Minister just laughed at him.

The SSG leader, who calls himself Hamish McNasty, said this afternoon, "Any English tourists who try to cross the border this Easter will be our target. We will crush their caravans, we will batter their buses, we will terrorise them in their tents and we will hit them with poisoned haggis in their hotels. And any tourists who do get through will return home to South Britain to find their houses are rubble. They shall not pass! We will show your Prime Minister that we mean business. We'll see who's laughing by Easter Monday!"

31

Roads to Scotland have been jammed with terrified tourists trying to turn round and head back home. As one frightened family said, "We shall be holidaying at home this Easter. We will defend 23 Cabbage Patch Road, Duckpool, to the death!"

guest-houses in Scotland are empty. "This could well be a disaster!" one Lanarkshire landlady lamented.

There are no reports of any attacks, but panic has hit the highways on the first evening of the holidays. Most Scots people are puzzled as to who this Separate Scotland Group might be. Where do they live? What do they hope to gain? But one thing's for certain – hotels and

Police on both sides of the border are trying to track down Mr McNasty. "Of course that might not be his real name," said Chief Constable Nutter of Northumbria police.

Our reporter asked the Chief Constable if McNasty could be some kind of Nutter. The policeman replied, "I don't think we have anyone in our family like that."

But it wasn't an old wartime newspaper – the date was today's!

"It's happening all over again!" Gary Grint whispered while Miss Monument went to fetch the books. "The English are fleeing from Scotland because they're afraid of what'll happen to their homes while they're away. That's just what the Romans did back in the year AD410."

"Did someone threaten to crush their caravans?" Pete Plank asked.

"No. But groups of barbarians called Goths started to attack Rome," he said, pulling papers from inside his creaking leather satchel. "I have my own research here," he said.

"Tell us what you know, short-sighted-but-clever boy!" Mabel ordered.

Gary pushed his spectacles back on his nose and said. "As you know, the Romans ruled England for nearly four hundred years. But, in AD410 there came a famous message from their Emperor Honorius..."

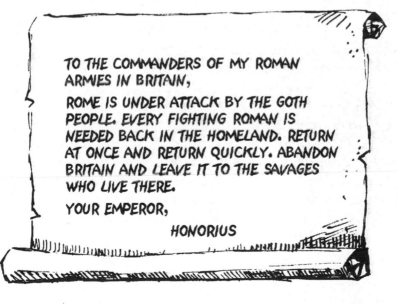

TO THE COMMANDERS OF MY ROMAN ARMIES IN BRITAIN,

ROME IS UNDER ATTACK BY THE GOTH PEOPLE. EVERY FIGHTING ROMAN IS NEEDED BACK IN THE HOMELAND. RETURN AT ONCE AND RETURN QUICKLY. ABANDON BRITAIN AND LEAVE IT TO THE SAVAGES WHO LIVE THERE.

YOUR EMPEROR,

HONORIUS

"Just imagine!" Gary breathed. "For hundreds of years you've had the Roman army to look after you. They drove the Picts and Scots back to Scotland, the Irish back to Ireland and the Saxons back to Denmark. Now your protectors disappear. What happens next?"

"The enemies start to attack again," I said grimly. "And what can you do about it?" I asked.

"Run away," Gary said. Gary would say that. "But Britain is an island. You can't run for ever. Look what one abandoned Briton wrote..."

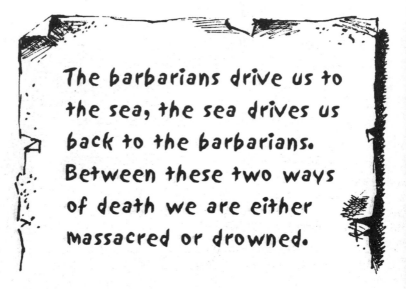

The barbarians drive us to the sea, the sea drives us back to the barbarians. Between these two ways of death we are either massacred or drowned.

Pete Plank shook his head. "I wouldn't let them push me into the sea and I wouldn't let them massacre me!" he said. "I would fight!"

Gary squinted at Pete. "Brave words, Peter, brave words. You can just imagine a bold young man saying those words fifteen hundred years ago! And that man was called Arthur! The real King Arthur!"

"That's me!" Pete said proudly.

"Less than a hundred years after the Romans left, the Britons began to fight back!" Gary told him.

Pete stood up and waved the *Duckpool Daily News* like a sword. "Let's savage those Saxons! Let's stuff the Scots! Let's fight for freedom! Follow me! I am Arthur and I will lead you in the great battles!"

It was a good, exciting story; it was even better than our play because it was true... at least I thought it was. I could see what he meant. "What we need is a new Arthur! Someone to lead us against these invaders!"

There was a cough from the doorway and Mildred Monument stood there with an armful of books. "The books!" she said.

Gary smiled at her. "Have you a copy of the book by Nennius?"

The librarian placed the books on the table. First came the rules...

I wanted to ask if it was all right to breathe but decided she'd just say "no" and put my head in a paper bag.

Gary took an old book from the table as gently as if it were a baby. "These are the writings of Nennius," he explained. "He was the first person to write about a king called Arthur."

Miss Monument pointed a bony finger at the old man. "No!" she said. "You need to read all the histories from those times. The writings of Gildas and Bede. Nennius may have been the first to mention Arthur. But what about Bede and Gildas, eh? They came before Nennius. I hope you aren't scared to show your friends those too?"

Gary spread his hands. "The knights of King Arthur are never scared of the truth," he said.

And I suppose that's when I realised the play and the legend had stopped being separate things. Gary had called us "the knights of King Arthur" ...and I could see my Time Detectives team just loved the idea.

Chapter 5
A Bede and a border

Miss Monument's eyes glinted behind the thick lenses of her glasses and she opened a book that was yellow with age.

"Gildas!" she said.

"Bless you," I muttered.

"This Gildas is a man who was writing in AD540 so he was alive at the same time as your Arthur was supposed to live. You'd believe him, wouldn't you?"

"Probably," I nodded. "What does he say about Arthur?"

Miss Monument let her little mouth open in a show of sharp little teeth. "Nothing!" she cackled. "Heh! Heh! That's the problem! Nothing!"

She waved the book under my nose...

Gary gave the frosty librarian a sunshine smile that failed to melt her. "Ah, but look at this page," he said.

The ruin of Britain
by
Gildas

The Romans left and the Britons were invaded by the tribes from the north. Britons fought against Britons, crops were not gathered and there was terrible famine. The Britons invited Saxons from over the sea to defend them. The Saxons fought well but soon turned on the Britons and killed the people who had invited them to Britain.

Many rich Britons ran away to their lands over the sea in Gaul. But one leader stayed and gave heart to the Britons. That man came from a Roman family who had stayed behind and his name was Ambrosius Aurelianus. This great warrior was maybe the last of the Romans to survive.

Ambrosius Aurelianus won great victories against the northern invaders and the Saxons. He conquered the tyrants of the west, he conquered Conan of Gloucester, he conquered the three wicked kings of Wales. His greatest victory was at Mount Badon where he even conquered the Saxons.
But even this did not bring peace.

"Maybe he ran out of conkers," Pete Plank sighed.

Miss Monument looked as if she had conquered us all. "See? No mention of Arthur!"

Gary just grinned and spread his hands. "No, but Ambrosius Aurelianus was just the king; Arthur was the general who led the battle! Gildas does go on to write about a great leader who brought lasting peace. He doesn't name him Arthur, but that's who he meant."

She frowned at him and thrust another book under his nose. "So look at England's first great historian. His name was Bede and he wrote this history..."

The disaster at Hadrian's Wall

When the wall was finished the Romans showed the Britons how to defend it from attacks by the Picts and the Scots in the north. But the Romans soon said goodbye to their friends and never returned.

The gloomy British soldiers lived in terror day and night. Beyond that wall the Picts and the Scots constantly attacked them with hooked weapons. They dragged the defenders down from Hadrian's Wall and dashed them to the ground. At last the Britons abandoned their cities and the wall and fled in panic and confusion.

"No mention of your Arthur there, either," the librarian murmured. "And Bede is your greatest historian."

"Not that great," Gary sniffed. "He made some terrible mistakes!"

Miss Monument's grey face turned a purple shade of pink. "It's here in Bede's book, you little toad of a boy. How dare you call the great Bede wrong? He says the pathetic little Britons fled from the mighty Scots and that's what happened..."

I held up a hand. "Let our Time Detective speak."

The librarian clamped her lips together and glared at Gary. Gary pointed to the book then looked up at her.

"Bede says the Romans finished the wall and then straight away left the Britons to defend it. But it didn't happen like that at all. Our teacher, Miss Toon, says the Romans built Hadrian's Wall around AD120 and we know the Romans didn't leave until AD410. That's almost three hundred years later! That's not 'soon after' the wall was finished, is it? That's one thing the Time Detectives have learned... just cos something's written in a book, it doesn't mean it has to be true! Bede is bonkers!"

"You tell her, Gary," I cheered.

The librarian raised two thick eyebrows over the wire rims of her glasses. "I can see you young Time Detectives are quite brilliant at following clues," she hissed. "But you still haven't proved Arthur existed."

"I hope he does exist," I said. "From those newspaper reports it looks as if we're going to need him. History is repeating itself all over again! That newspaper report on the Scottish Border trouble! The Picts and the Scots are threatening the Britons to the south of the border and the South Britons are panicking and running away!"

Gary nodded, pleased. "And, as I said, the only person to stop them is Arthur."

"We have to find him first!" Miss Monument reminded us.

"He's dead!" Pete said. "People don't fight very well when they're dead, Gary!"

The librarian's face split with a shark smile. "Or maybe he's only sleeping. That's why we're here. To find out if he's really dead and to track him down, wake him up!"

Gary turned to the librarian. "You can leave us with these books, if you like. If we find anything interesting we'll let you know."

She glared at him but started collecting books from a trolley marked 'Returns'. "I've a lot to do anyway. I will be back to close up at six thirty."

"What time is it now?" Pete asked.

Miss Monument didn't answer. Instead she snapped the switch on an old radio that was being used as a book shelf. We listened as the pips sounded the hour...

And with the time at six o'clock here is the Duckpool Radio news at...

...er ...ten seconds past six ... well actually it's fifteen seconds now because it took me five seconds to say, "Er... ten seconds past six," if you see what I mean. Anyway, here is the latest from our re-border on the porter... sorry, I'll say that again.
Our reporter on the Border.

Here on the old Border between England and Scotland the traffic chaos continues. In the east the bridge over the Tyne at Newcastle was at a standstill as caravan drivers tried to turn around and head back. Chief Constable Nutter of Northumbria police told them not to be stupid. So the caravans that had turned back turned back again so they were turned forward and ran into the caravans that had turned back... if you see what I mean.

And here on the west coast the M6 motorway is just as bad, as motorists, lorries, buses and caravans tried to cross the central reservation and ran into speeding traffic fleeing south from Scotland. Cumbria police say it could take days to sort out the mess. The Separate Scotland Group have sent an e-mail to say their army could attack any time this weekend, but probably Easter Saturday because it looks like being a nice day.

The radio returned to playing music and I turned to my team.

"Less than twenty-four hours to save South Britain!" I told my Time Detectives grimly.

Chapter 6
Nennius the ninny and other meddling monks

Gary opened the old book in the leather covers. "This is where the story of Arthur really starts," he said. "With the writings of a monk called Nennius."

"Nennius was a historian?" I asked.

Gary's button nose curled back. "I would hardly call him that," he sneered. "He was a monk."

"Do excuse me," Mabel said. "But if he was a monk he was a man of God and he must have been telling the truth."

Gary sighed and said, "First rule of Time Detectives: don't believe everything you read in books. Nennius may have been a monk but you'll find a lot of monks were fools and liars when they tell the story of Arthur."

Mabel jabbed a finger at him. "We are a Time Detectives team," she said. "Don't try to tell us what to think, you goggle-eyed boy."

Gary shrugged. "So, make up your own minds. Nennius the ninny wrote this *History of Britain* around the year 800. That was in the Dark Ages, of course."

"Uhh?" Pete grunted. "Why were they called the Dark Ages?" he asked.

"Cos there were lots of knights!" I said, quick as a frog in a frying pan. Gary groaned, Mabel looked disgusted and Gary chuckled. Pete just looked blank. "Dark nights – knights – geddit?" I asked.

"No, Katie," he said.

Mabel looked vinegar-drinking sour. "There is no time to waste with jokes if you're going to save South Britain."

Gary tapped the Nennius book. "Do you want to see what the man wrote?" he asked.

We nodded and he opened the book. Gary leaned over and read the old print in a language we could understand...

The chief of all the British chiefs, the king of Britain, was Arthur. In the eighth battle he painted the image of Holy Mary on his shield and fought the enemy boldly. At the Battle of Mount Badon 960 men fell at a single charge.

"Of course Nennius was writing two hundred years after the Battle of Mount Badon," Gary explained. "But another history called *The Welsh Annals* mentions Arthur twice. Look!" he said pointing to the next ancient book...

Arthur led the Britons at Mount Badon. He fought for three days and three nights and all that time he carried the cross of Our Lord Jesus Christ. But at the Battle of Camlann, nineteen years later, Arthur perished.

"So there you have it!" he said. "Less than two hundred years after he died there are two histories where King Arthur is mentioned: three if you count Gildas."

"But none of them tell us what happened to him," I moaned. "If we're going to wake him up then we have to know where he's buried!"

"And we'll need a really, really big alarm clock," Pete added.

Mabel's face twisted in disgust. "Sometimes you say the most stupid things, Pete Plank."

Pete frowned. "Uhh? He's been asleep a thousand years or more. So, how are we going to wake him up without a really, really big alarm clock?"

Mabel blinked. "Pour water over his face," she suggested. "A bucketful should do it."

A bucket over Mabel's head seemed like a better idea. "Look! Can we just find him first?" I asked. "We can worry about waking him up later. Where on earth is he buried?"

"Or where *in* earth is he buried?" Mabel joked. Her jokes were never very good.

Gary nodded. "After those three histories the next mention of Arthur is another three hundred years later. A Welsh monk called Geoffrey of Monmouth wrote all about him. Look... he wrote his *History of the Kings of Britain* around the year 1138..."

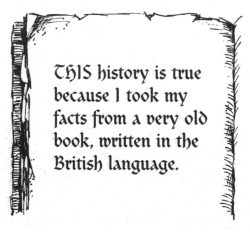

THIS history is true because I took my facts from a very old book, written in the British language.

Geoffrey said "The greatest king of the Britons was Arthur. This king, protected by the magician Merlin, ruled over a wonderful court in the southwest of Britain, the part we now call Cornwall.

After his final battle, at a place called Camlann, Arthur went to the island of Avalon, where his wounds healed and where he sleeps still, waiting to rescue Britain when danger comes."

"Do excuse me," Mabel said, "but that is absolutely useless!" She turned the pages. "This Geoffrey of Monmouth chap doesn't tell us where Camlann is!"

"Save yourself the trouble looking," Miss Monument said, walking back into the room. "After two weeks of research I haven't been able to find it on even the oldest maps. I despair! Perhaps there is no such place as Camlann. Perhaps Arthur is dead. Look at what William of Newburgh wrote in 1190, just fifty years after your precious Geoffrey of Monmouth finished his hopeless history."

The librarian opened another book and pointed with a hooked-claw of a finger at the piece she wanted us to read...

It is quite clear that everything Geoffrey of Monmouth wrote about Arthur was made up. Geoffrey only wrote it to please the king. There is no truth in his history of Arthur.

"See?" the woman crowed. "He reckons Geoffrey of Monmouth was just another mad monk trying to fool people into believing that Arthur's your great British hero."

"You haven't read the book by William of Malmesbury, have you?" Gary asked her.

For the first time Miss Monument looked a little uncertain. "No... but..."

"Get that for me and I'll show you where most people think Arthur is buried," he said.

"You can tell me the answer?" the librarian gasped. "You wonderful boy! I'll see if we have the Malmesbury book in the library."

She swept out of the room in a swirl of cardigan and kilt.

"Hey!" Gary cried. "Maybe I could find a copy of Malmesbury on the internet. This computer's linked to a phone line," he said, pointing to the machine in the corner.

"Give it a try, Gary," I told him.

He grabbed the mouse and with a few clicks he brought up the internet programme. Then he stopped and gave a low whistle.

"What's wrong?" Mabel asked sharply. "Do hurry up or that nice lady may return and be very annoyed. If she tells Daddy we've misused council property then I will be in frightful trouble."

"Mabel, close your frightful mouth and listen to what Gary has to say," I ordered. "What have you found, Gary?"

"Every time you go on the internet, you leave a record on the computer – it's called a 'history'. Look at the last thing someone was reading on this computer," he said, and clicked a button. The screen changed and it was our turn to whistle. We must have sounded like a cage full of canaries.

THE SEPARATE SCOTLAND HOME PAGE

Welcome friends of Scotland. Our plan to separate us from the evil English has started well. They have panicked and blocked their roads already. This means their tanks and troop carriers will not be able to get through to the Border.

The cowardly English have made their own road blocks! Ha!

Our army of 10,000 Scots can march into England tomorrow and we'll be there before they can stop us!

Strength to the Scots and the terrible tartan army!

"Why does someone in Duckpool Library want to read about the Separate Scotland Group?" I asked.

"Does the government know there's an army of 10,000 on its way?" Gary asked.

"How can we stop them?" I asked.

But it was Pete Plank who asked the most sensible question. "Why can't our soldiers just fly over the road blocks in helicopters?" he muttered.

"Why don't we do just that?" Mabel cried.

Chapter 7
Burials and bones

I looked at Mabel Tweed sourly. "Mabel, we don't have a helicopter."

She used a little finger to brush her plucked eyebrow and look pleased with herself. "Daddy does. He's a millionaire, you know? If I ask him nicely then I can borrow it!"

"William of Malmesbury!" Miss Monument cried, coming back into the room with a book held in front of her like a great golden tea-tray. "Another monk."

Gary blinked behind his spectacles and licked his lips. He tapped the book. "Not only does it show you where Arthur was buried it also shows you he is dead. There will be no King Arthur coming to the rescue of you South Britons..."

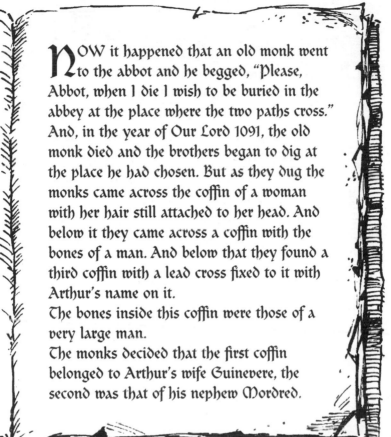

NOW it happened that an old monk went to the abbot and he begged, "Please, Abbot, when I die I wish to be buried in the abbey at the place where the two paths cross." And, in the year of Our Lord 1091, the old monk died and the brothers began to dig at the place he had chosen. But as they dug the monks came across the coffin of a woman with her hair still attached to her head. And below it they came across a coffin with the bones of a man. And below that they found a third coffin with a lead cross fixed to it with Arthur's name on it.

The bones inside this coffin were those of a very large man.

The monks decided that the first coffin belonged to Arthur's wife Guinevere, the second was that of his nephew Mordred.

Miss Mildred Monument looked pleased with herself. I was surprised that our Time Detective, Mabel, was so keen to support her. "Do excuse me, Katie," Mabel sneered. "But it does look as if that play of yours was just a fairy tale after all. Arthur is dead as a duck's toenail!"

"That's what a visitor to the abbey said," Miss Monument put in. "His name was Gerald of Wales. He saw the cross and the bones and he wrote this...

It is clear that the stories of Arthur being carried away to a distant island are nonsense. There most certainly is a body here and it is most certainly Arthur's. When it was discovered there were miracles and wonderful signs. The bones were taken into the church and laid to rest again.

Gary looked thoughtful. "What happened to the cross?" he asked.

The librarian took a small leaflet from the pile of books. "It tells you here in this guide to Glastonbury. The cross disappeared two hundred years ago... but

a man called Camden drew a picture of it... look."

"Uhh?" Pete Plank gasped. "That writing's even worse than mine! Those monks could do with some lessons from Miss Toon!"

"Oh, really!" Mabel exploded. She gave the librarian a sickly smile. "You see the sort of people I have to do my Time Detective work with? He doesn't even know it's written in the monks' own language."

Miss Monument looked pleased. "That is correct, Miss Tweed. It's written in Latin!"

"So what does it say, smarty-knickers Tweed?" I asked the millionaire's miserable daughter.

The librarian said quickly, "It says, 'Here lies the famous King Arthur, buried in the Isle of Avalon.' See! It looks like he could be dead!"

"That cross disappeared," I said. "But the bones must still be there."

The librarian turned the page of the guidebook and pointed to the next section...

ARTHUR'S GRAVE IS OPENED

In the year 1278 King Edward I visited Glastonbury with his wife, Queen Eleanor.

On Easter Tuesday the grave of Arthur was opened to show Edward the ancient hero. Inside were two bones of wonderful size and the delicate bones of the queen.

The next day, Easter Wednesday, the king and queen wrapped the bones and moved them to a black marble tomb. The tomb was sealed. The cover of this tomb survived until King Henry VIII had the monastery destroyed in 1539.

Then, in 1931, historians dug at the site of the tomb, hoping to find the bones. They found a tomb beneath the ground, but it was quite, quite empty!

SITE OF KING ARTHUR'S TOMB

GLASTONBURY TOR

"Now listen, everyone," Mabel said. "I suggest that I take Daddy's helicopter and fly over to Glastonbury and see what I can find. We've done all we can with these books and now it's time to do a spot of research on the spot, to see what I can spot."

"Any more spots and you'll look like a giraffe," I muttered.

Miss Monument lunged forward and grabbed Mabel by the arm. "A helicopter! You have a helicopter! Then why don't I come with you, dear girl? I've always wanted to visit the old monastery! I am fascinated by ancient monuments."

"She must spend a lot of time looking in mirrors, then," I said, nudging Pete. I thought that was quite a clever thing to say. Miss Monument, ancient monument, see? I waited for Pete to fall off his chair with laughter.

He said, "Uhh?"

Never mind.

Chapter 8
Bombs and bagpipes

The librarian hustled us out onto the darkening street and locked the library. She set off with Mabel, planning their helicopter trip and ignoring the rest of us.

Suddenly there was a screaming wail and I had to cover my ears. The library windows shook and bats fell off their perches in the tower. "What's that?" I cried, as the ghost-wail faded.

Gary looked grim. "I remember hearing that in a television programme, Katie. That was an air-raid siren. Not heard that since the last war! It warns you when a bombing raid's about to happen. Someone's getting pretty scared by this threat of a war!"

"But I thought that was up north near Hadrian's Wall," I argued.

"That's what I thought," Gary said

Pete began to wheel his motorbike down the street. "It looks as if we're too late to save South Britain."

Pete, Gary and I trudged towards the High Street where a crowd of people were clustered round the window of the television shop. We could see the pictures on twenty screens and everyone was so silent we could hear the sound from inside the shop...

Tonight the Separate Scotland Group contacted the Duckpool Evening News service with the following message: "We want Scotland for the Scots. All Scottish schools will have bagpipe lessons every day and haggis for school dinner. Next week there are the elections to the new Scottish parliament. Vote for us and we will throw out the English invaders. If they want to come here they'll need passports."

Unfortunately we are not allowed to read that message to you because the British Government say it is just a cheap advert for votes in the elections. So please forget we ever said it.

And the Duckpool Television plane has flown over the Border region where an army of 10,000 is supposed to be invading somewhere. So far we have been unable to see any troops anywhere. This could be because they have perfect camouflage, of course. But we did get some lovely pictures of spring lambs playing in the heather. We also got smashing pictures of the tangle of cars and caravans on the northern roads and you should see the punch-ups on the Tyne Bridge! Wow!

The Time detectives said gloomy goodnights and split. So I was surprised to get a phone call from Gary just as I was going to bed.

"Are you asleep yet, Katie?" he asked in a whisper.

"No, Gary, but I'm lying on the edge of the bed so I'll soon drop off."

"Listen! I've done some internet research. Switch your computer on and look at the information I've sent by e-mail. I'll call you back in ten minutes!"

He put the phone down. I yawned but did what he asked. And I found his message...

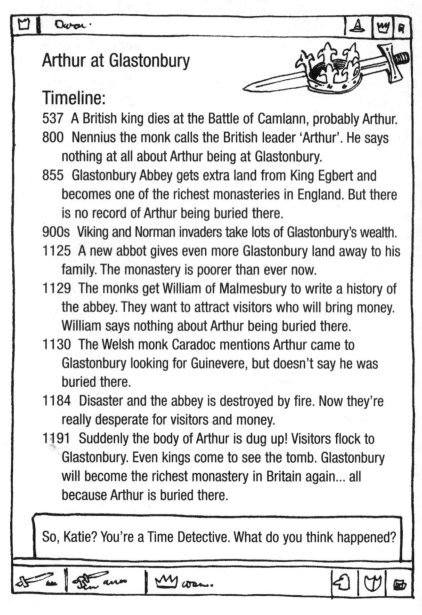

Arthur at Glastonbury

Timeline:

537 A British king dies at the Battle of Camlann, probably Arthur.

800 Nennius the monk calls the British leader 'Arthur'. He says nothing at all about Arthur being at Glastonbury.

855 Glastonbury Abbey gets extra land from King Egbert and becomes one of the richest monasteries in England. But there is no record of Arthur being buried there.

900s Viking and Norman invaders take lots of Glastonbury's wealth.

1125 A new abbot gives even more Glastonbury land away to his family. The monastery is poorer than ever now.

1129 The monks get William of Malmesbury to write a history of the abbey. They want to attract visitors who will bring money. William says nothing about Arthur being buried there.

1130 The Welsh monk Caradoc mentions Arthur came to Glastonbury looking for Guinevere, but doesn't say he was buried there.

1184 Disaster and the abbey is destroyed by fire. Now they're really desperate for visitors and money.

1191 Suddenly the body of Arthur is dug up! Visitors flock to Glastonbury. Even kings come to see the tomb. Glastonbury will become the richest monastery in Britain again... all because Arthur is buried there.

So, Katie? You're a Time Detective. What do you think happened?

And that's just what he asked me when the phone rang ten minutes later and I'd had time to think about it. The line buzzed and clicked. I had to shout to make myself heard.

"Arthur was never buried at Glastonbury," I said excitedly. "The monks wanted a great attraction to get visitors... like Blackpool has the Tower and London has the crown jewels. They faked it!" I told him.

"That's what I reckon," Gary said. "Mildred Monument's wrong. Arthur isn't dead and buried at Glastonbury after all. Arthur is buried somewhere else and he could be just sleeping! There's still a chance for us Katie!"

"Where?" I asked.

"There's also one other piece of evidence that I've uncovered," he said. "Arthur disappeared after the Battle of Camlann but no one has worked out where Camlann is."

"So what's the use of telling me that?" I asked him angrily.

Gary sounded really pleased with himself. If he'd been a cat he'd have been purring. "Maybe I've been able to work it out!"

"What!?!" I cried. "Where is it?"

"Arthur fought a lot of battles against the Scots on the Borders. He probably made his last stand somewhere on Hadrian's Wall."

"How long is Hadrian's Wall? Eighty miles? We can't search eighty miles before this next invasion!"

"But Katie!" he said excitedly. "The word Camlann means 'crooked valley'. And, on Hadrian's Wall there's a deserted camp called Birdoswald. And guess what Birdoswald was called?"

"Camlann?" I guessed.

"Near enough! It was called Camboglanna, meaning 'crooked valley'! I reckon it means Arthur is buried somewhere near Birdoswald!"

The buzzing and clicking on the line was interrupted by a cruel laugh and a final click. "What was that, Gary?" I asked him.

"I think the phone line was tapped. Someone was listening to what we were saying," he said.

"So someone else knows where Arthur is! If that 'someone' supports the Separate Scotland Group they'll get there first and destroy Arthur's grave!" I moaned.

"If it exists," Gary said carefully.

"We have to go there!" I told him. "That's where everything is happening. I'll get Mabel to fly us there. She's wasting her time going to Glastonbury!"

I telephoned Mabel's home number. A snobbish voice answered, "This is Mayor Tweed's residence."

"Can I speak to Mabel – like now!" I said.

The man on the other end told me to wait and five minutes later he returned.

"I am sorry. But Miss Tweed has gone off with a Miss Mildred Monument in the mayor's helicopter."

"To Glastonbury?" I asked.

"No. Mayor Tweed's secretary said they headed north..." the man began.

"...and when you asked where they were going you were told Hadrian's Wall."

"How did you know that?" he asked.

"Cos I'm a Time Detective," I said, and slammed down the phone.

I called Pete Plank and tried to explain. "Miss Monument with her tartan skirt... we should have guessed she was a Separate Scotland Group member. Her strange accent... Scottish! The messages on her office computer... she was sending out all the news of an invasion!"

"But she was looking for the truth about Arthur!" he reminded me.

"Yes! She wanted to be sure there is no sleeping Arthur ready to wake up and stop this invasion! She's not interested in waking Arthur, she's interested in stopping us from waking him! I've got to get up there, Pete."

"The roads are blocked," he pointed out.

"But your motor-cycle could get through," I said.

And that's how I came to be sneaking out of the house an hour later. Pete Plank was waiting on the corner of the street as I'd told him to on the phone. Dressed in black shining leather and a helmet he could have been King Arthur on a motorbike. Under his arm he carried Miss Toon's window pole.

It wasn't much of a lance to fight the new Scots invaders. But, as I slipped on the spare helmet and climbed up behind him I decided it was the best we could do.

Arthur and his Guinevere rode out to Camlann and the last battle again.

Chapter 9
The last great battle of Arthur's heirs

We drove northwards through the night. The roads were busy with Easter traffic, with the early holidaymakers fleeing from Scotland and with late sightseers flying towards Scotland to see the battle.

We stopped for petrol using Pete's dad's credit card and grabbed a coffee at the service area to keep us awake. A television droned on in the snack bar with the latest news...

And at last there is some sign of activity on the old Scottish border at Birdoswald. A helicopter dropped a kilted figure onto a bulldozer. Observers saw a girl with ringlets and a white dress tied to the bulldozer as a hostage.

MENU
EGG + CHIPS
BACON + CHIPS
HAMBURGER + CHIPS
SAUSAGE + CHIPS
CHIPS + CHIPS

No one is able to get near to rescue the girl because the roads are still blocked by cars and caravans. But it seems the bulldozer is digging a deep moat on the Scottish side of the Roman wall.

When the dozer-driver was asked what he was doing, he replied, "Separating Scotland! We beat your King Arthur once and we'll be free of you South Britons again!" Meanwhile, the helicopter which brought the girl and the Scot has been identified as that of Mayor Walter Tweed of Duckpool.

"It is possible that the girl is Mayor Tweed's daughter, Mabel," Police Chief Nutter said. "Sadly there's no King Arthur to free this maiden in distress!" If the British army tries to attack then the Scot has threatened to dump the girl in the ditch! It looks as if the Separate Scotland Group have won!

"Hah! Not if we get there first!" I told Pete.

"Uhh?" he grunted. "What can we do, Katie?"

"Trust me, I know what I'm doing," I said... because the truth is I had no idea. "You'll see."

By the time we found Birdoswald the sun was up. The ancient ruin of the wall stretched east and west and disappeared into the morning mists.

Empty cars cluttered the lanes around with the passengers all gathered on Hadrian's Wall looking towards the north. Pete used all his motor-cycle skills to cross the fields, slip through a gap in the wall and head towards the roaring and clanking of the largest bulldozer you've ever seen.

It gleamed yellow in the sun and poured out clouds of filthy diesel fumes. The ditch was wide and deep and beginning to fill with water from the wet fields around.

69

The Scot at the controls had thrown off his wig and the cardigan and thrown out the tombstone false teeth. But he kept the kilt. Miss Mildred Monument was the dreaded Hamish McNasty after all!

Mabel was tied to the corner of the cab and looked absolutely furious. She was struggling with the rope and it was already loose around her waist.

McNasty caught sight of Pete and me on the motorbike and swung the bulldozer to face us. There was a clear patch of grass between the machine and us. It was perfect for a knightly charge.

I lowered my wooden window pole and clutched tightly to Pete's leather jacket.

The savage Scot laughed and grabbed a piece of scaffolding pole. His shield was the mighty scoop of the bulldozer.

"We haven't found Arthur!" Pete said.

"He could be dead, Pete... but his spirit is still alive!"

"Where is it?" he asked.

"It's inside you, Pete. When Britain faces her greatest danger then Arthur might not wake up, but his spirit has to! It's up to us, Pete. You're Arthur, I'm Guinevere. Let's fight!"

"Doesn't look a very fair fight," Pete called over the revving of the motorbike.

"Trust me, I know what I'm doing!" I shouted through the helmet. "Arthur's here, Pete. He's somewhere here and if he hasn't shown up himself it's because he knows he can trust us to do the job!"

I slapped his shoulder, he lowered his visor and I lowered my lance.

What happened next you'll have seen on the famous news videos. People with cameras lined the ancient wall and caught the action. If I hadn't seen it for myself I'd never have believed it...

At the moment we set off Mabel, pushed free of the rope loop and stretched up her hands. The waiting helicopter swooped down and lowered a loop.

Mabel slipped her foot into the loop and was lifted clear of the yellow machine as it rumbled forward.

Pete went faster, the bulldozer churned towards us. Two hundred metres became one hundred became fifty... and the scaffolding pole was aimed straight at Pete's helmet.

I knew it would go clean through and clean through both our heads too. Then Mabel seemed to slip. Her hands let go of the lifting rope...

I waited for her to tumble down to earth and be crushed under the bulldozer. But her foot was in the loop. She hung there. Upside down!

"Uhh!" Pete cried. "I never knew Mabel wore stripy knickers!"

"A real knight and a gentleman wouldn't look!" I shouted.

Twenty metres... and then it happened...

Still upside-down, Mabel seemed to reach down and grab at the metal pole. The helicopter rose at the same time and the pole was snatched upwards, out of our way.

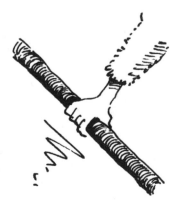

Ten metres... and I aimed my metal-tipped pole carefully and hit the windscreen of the bulldozer cab in the middle. It smashed into a million pieces.

We sped past as my lance shattered and we skidded over the dew-damp grass. Somehow Pete got us to a safe stop.

We turned to see the bulldozer tumble into its own moat as Hamish McNasty jumped to save himself from being crushed. He landed in the water and rose spluttering, "I canna swim!"

At that moment Mabel and the helicopter swooped again. She reached down a hand, snatched the kilted man up and dropped him at the feet of the police who waited by the wall.

"Uhh!" Pete cried. "That Mildred Monument wasn't wearing no knickers, Katie! And she wasn't a woman!"

I raised my visor and sighed. "Not Mildred but Mordred. And this time Arthur won."

"Did I do well, Katie?" Pete asked shyly.

"You did brilliantly... now get us out of here before the police ask about your driving licence!"

Chapter 10
Arthur's marvellous medal

Miss Toon helped us to put the truth and the legends about King Arthur into some sort of order.

"You can go to Winchester and see King Arthur's Round Table," she said. "But that was just an idea of the king who lived 800 years after the real Arthur. He had a round table made for his knights, but it wasn't Arthur's table. Nothing of Arthur is around today, not his table or his Camelot Castle or his bones."

I wrapped an arm round Pete Plank's wide shoulders. "Just his spirit, Miss!"

Miss Toon knew the full story. She smiled at us. "Just his battling spirit, Katie. Whenever someone stands up to a bully then Arthur's spirit lives on."

The teacher looked at her watch. "Which reminds me. It's time to go into the hall. There's a little presentation to be made..."

It was all a mystery to me. It was also a huge surprise to troop into the hall and see Mr Potty Potterton the headteacher there on the stage. He was flapping his hands and excited and terrified and pleased and confused all at the same time. I soon saw why. Sitting on the stage behind him, in the headteacher's armchair, was the Queen.

You probably remember seeing that on the news too...

I was shocked and pleased and embarrassed. I'd have to make a speech... I'd have to remember to mention the parts played by Pete and Gary. Even Mabel deserved a little mention. I might even get a day off school to have my picture taken and reporters to record my life story.

In my dreamy state I hardly heard the Queen's speech... but it's here on video...

There never was a Separate Scotland Group, just one man who used all the power of computers to deceive us. But our heroine didn't know that when she set out to do battle with him. And if Britain lives for a thousand years, men will still say, 'This was their finest hour.' Never in the field of human conflict was so much owed by so many to one brave girl!

I'll swear I was blushing poppy red! I began to sit up, ready to walk forward to receive this honour. I felt the smile spreading over my face as the Queen said...

"Never mind," Gary said later as we stood in the
playground and waved the royal Rolls Royce away.
"King Arthur didn't have the truth told about him
either."

"I never wanted a medal anyway," I sniffed.

"Yeah," Gary nodded. "The best heroes are
always the secret heroes."

Time trail

AD410   The Romans leave Britain. They've got a lot of
        problems back home and, as they say, "There's no
        place like Rome." Britain is defenceless. The
        Angles and the Saxons come over the North Sea
        and batter the Brits. The old Roman towns fall
        into ruins.

AD500   The Brits at last fight back. Sadly they are
        defeated in a great battle at Mons Badonicus
        (That's Mount Badon to you and me). The Brits
        are led by someone whose family were left behind
        by the Romans. And his name is Arthur. Great
        news for the battling Brits to have a leader like
        him but...

AD537   Arthur is killed. Some people believe he died near
        Hadrian's Wall, the old border between England
        and Scotland. He could become just another
        conquered king but ...

AD800   A Welsh monk Nennius writes his History of
         Britain and mentions a British king called Arthur
         who fought 12 great battles against invaders.
         And...

1135   A Welsh monk called Geoffrey of Monmouth
         writes about Arthur. Not that old Geoff can
         remember Arthur personally, of course. And
         another writer says, "It is quite clear that
         everything Geoffrey wrote about Arthur was made
         up." Then...

1155   A poet called Wace tells Arthur's story and
         mentions the Round Table.

1160   Another story-teller, Chretien de Troyes, adds bits
         to the story to make Arthur seem like a knight in
         armour, not just a British warrior.

1190 Now a poet called Robert be Boron adds the bit about Arthur's knights and the Holy Grail. People who drink from that can live forever. So...

1200-ish An English priest adds that Arthur isn't dead, just sleeping. He'll be back when England is threatened again.

2000 Britain is still fascinated by the story of Arthur. SO much that the Queen names her son the Prince of Wales Charles... and gives him a middle name: Arthur!